THE MYSTERIES OF
HARRIS BURDICK

CHRIS VAN ALLSBURG

HOUGHTON MIFFLIN COMPANY

BOSTON

With thanks to
Peter Wenders

Library of Congress Cataloging in Publication Data

Van Allsburg, Chris.
    The mysteries of Harris Burdick.

    Summary: Presents a series of loosely related drawings
each accompanied by a title and a caption which the
reader may use to make up his or her own story.
    1. Plot-your-own stories. 2. Children's stories,
American. {1. Mystery and detective stories. 2. Plot-
your-own stories}   I. Title.
PZ7.V266My   1984   [Fic]   84-9006
ISBN 0-395-35393-9

Printed in the United States of America

LBM 30 29 28 27 26 25 24 23 22 21

INTRODUCTION

I first saw the drawings in this book a year ago, in the home of a man named Peter Wenders. Though Mr. Wenders is retired now, he once worked for a children's book publisher, choosing the stories and pictures that would be turned into books.

Thirty years ago a man called at Peter Wenders's office, introducing himself as Harris Burdick. Mr. Burdick explained that he had written fourteen stories and had drawn many pictures for each one. He'd brought with him just one drawing from each story, to see if Wenders liked his work.

Peter Wenders was fascinated by the drawings. He told Burdick he would like to read the stories that went with them as soon as possible. The artist agreed to bring the stories the next morning. He left the fourteen drawings with Wenders. But he did not return the next day. Or the day after that. Harris Burdick was never heard from again. Over the years, Wenders tried to find out who Burdick was and what had happened to him, but he discovered nothing. To this day Harris Burdick remains a complete mystery.

His disappearance is not the only mystery left behind. What were the stories that went with these drawings? There are some clues. Burdick had written a title and caption for each picture. When I told Peter Wenders how difficult it was to look at the drawings and their captions without imagining a story, he smiled and left the room. He returned with a dust-covered cardboard box. Inside were dozens of stories, all inspired by the Burdick drawings. They'd been written years ago by Wenders's children and their friends.

I spent the rest of my visit reading these stories. They were remarkable, some bizarre, some funny, some downright scary. In the hope that other children will be inspired by them, the Burdick drawings are reproduced here for the first time.

Chris Van Allsburg
Providence, Rhode Island

ARCHIE SMITH, BOY WONDER

A tiny voice asked, "Is he the one?"

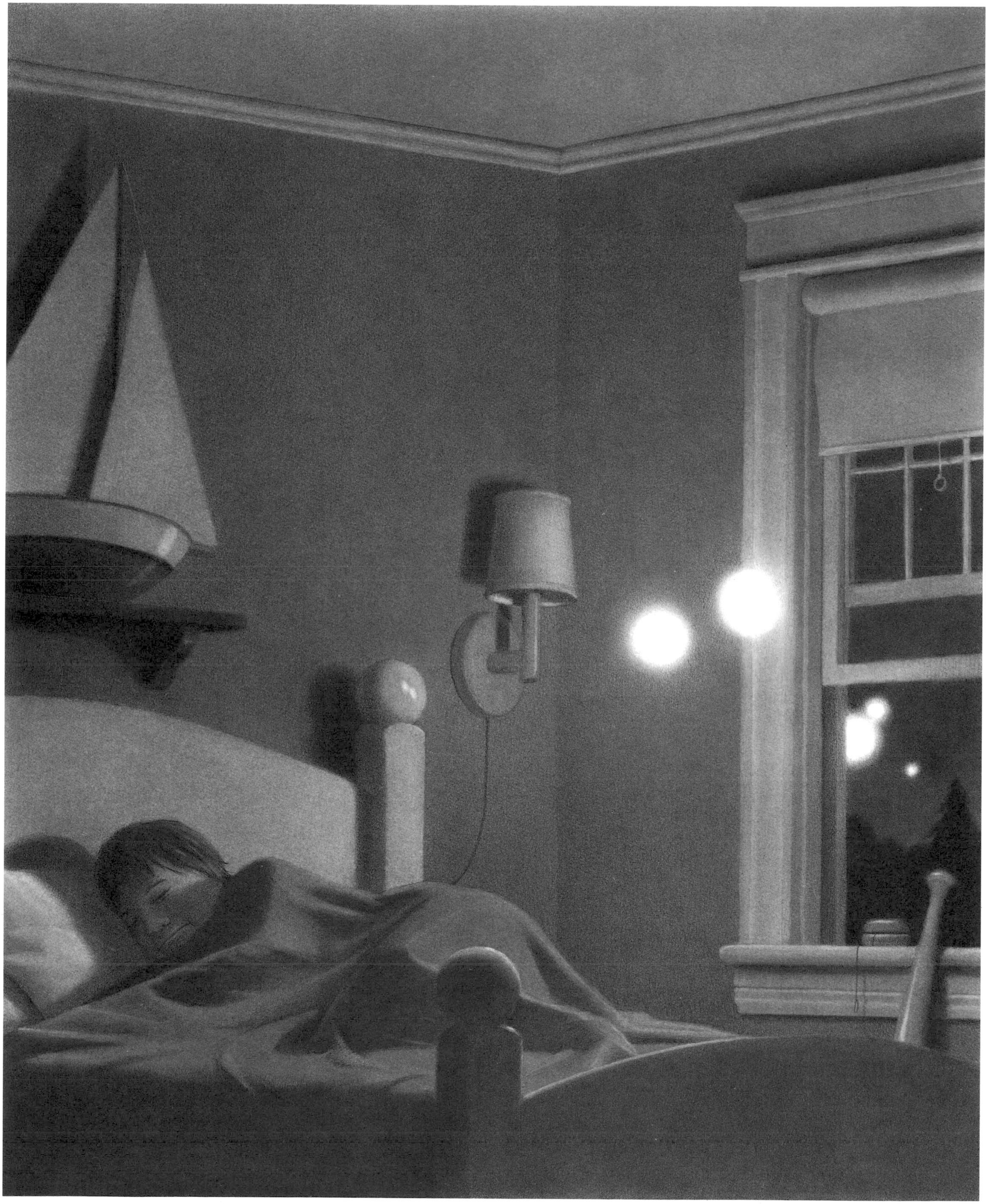

UNDER THE RUG

Two weeks passed and it happened again.

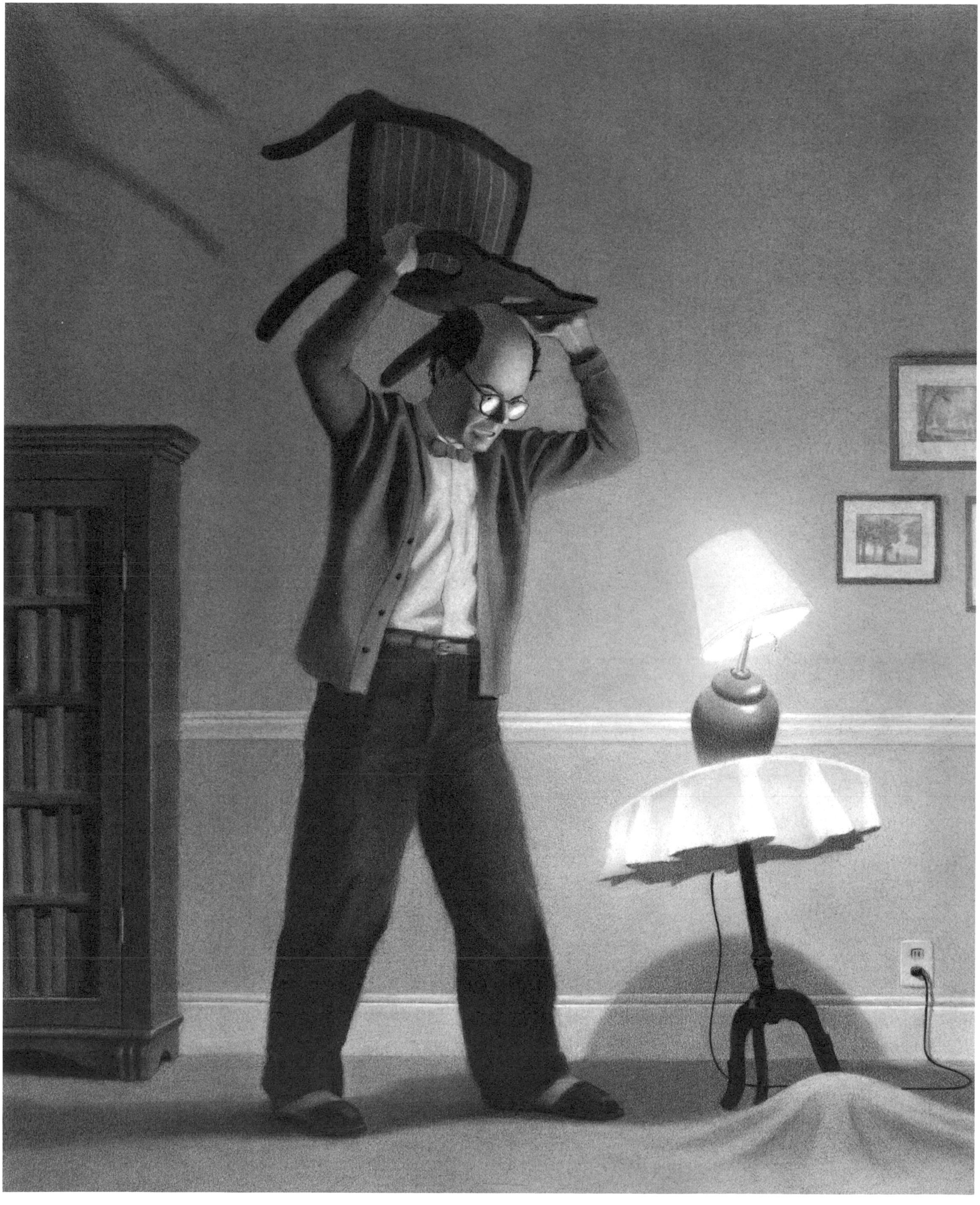

A STRANGE DAY IN JULY

He threw with all his might, but the
third stone came skipping back.

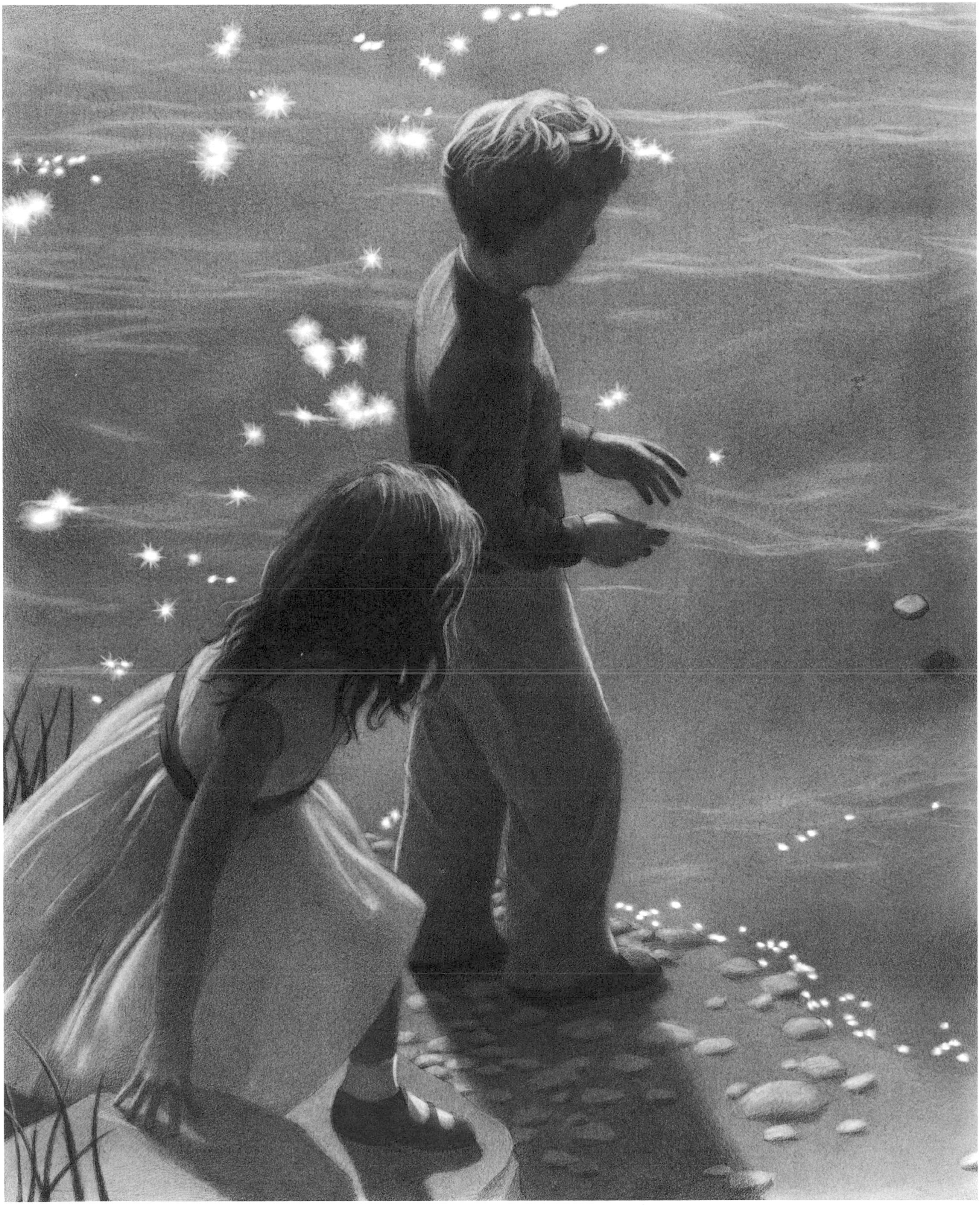

MISSING IN VENICE

*Even with her mighty engines in reverse,
the ocean liner was pulled further and
further into the canal.*

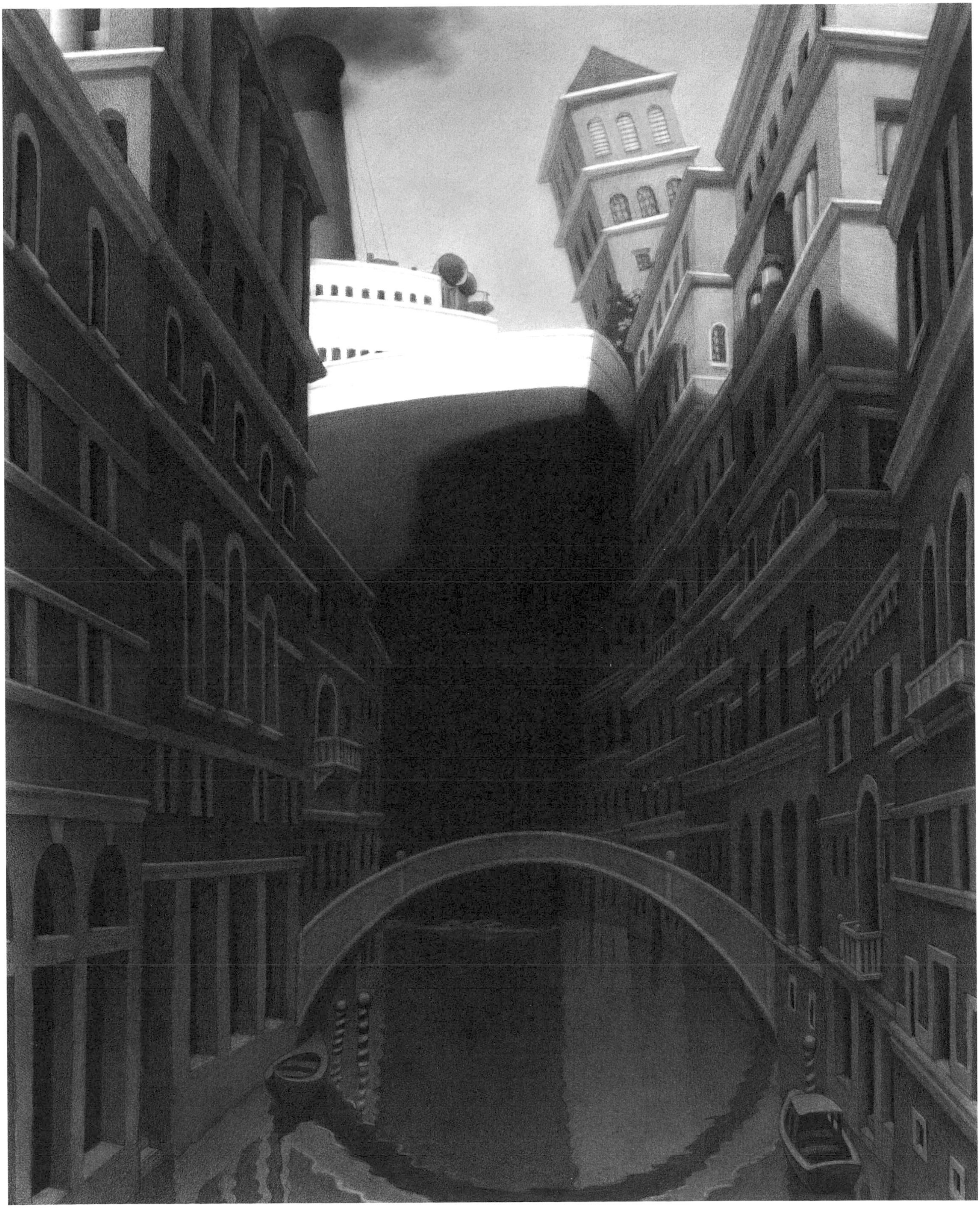

ANOTHER PLACE, ANOTHER TIME

If there was an answer, he'd find it there.

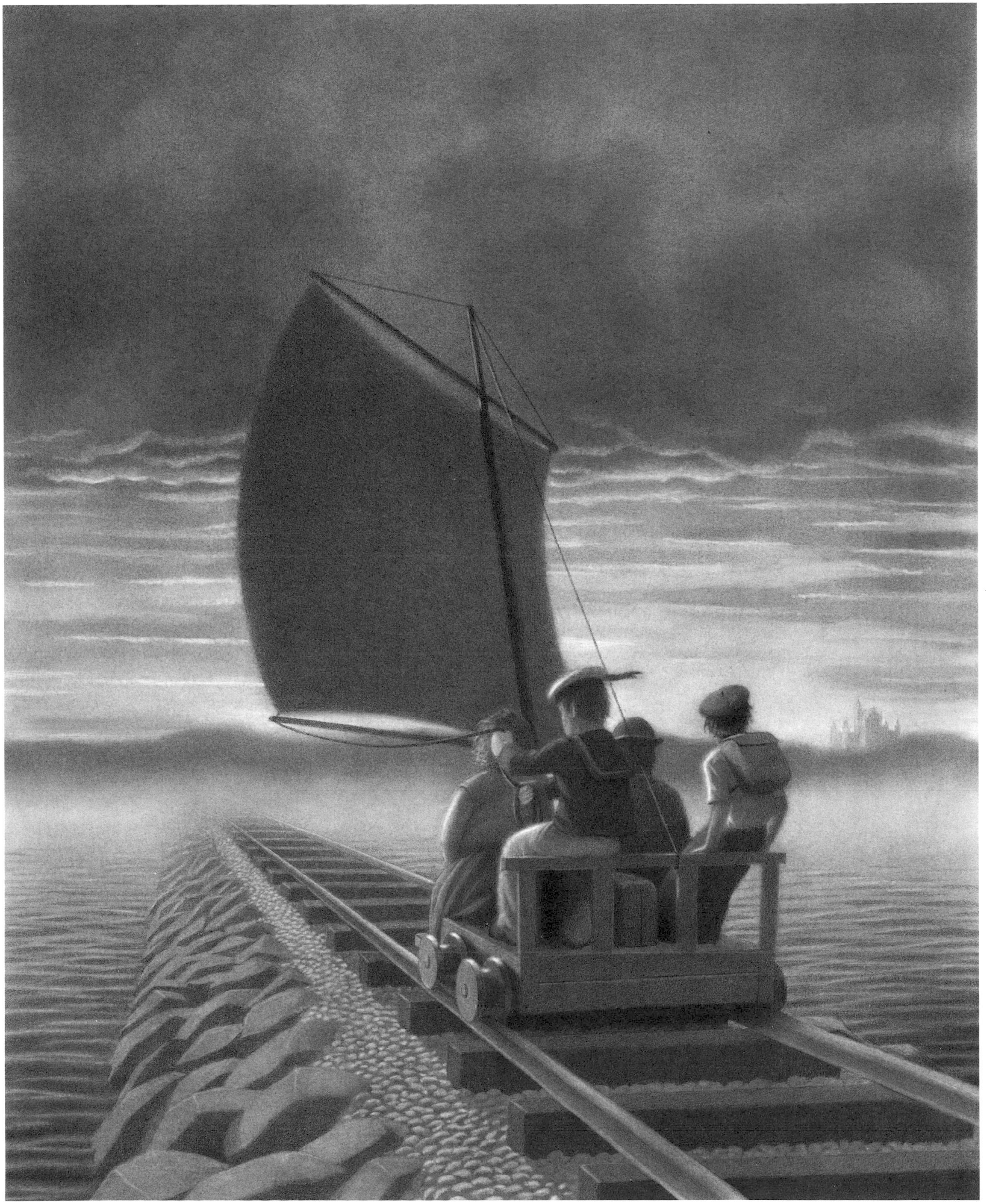

UNINVITED GUESTS

His heart was pounding.
He was sure he had seen the doorknob turn.

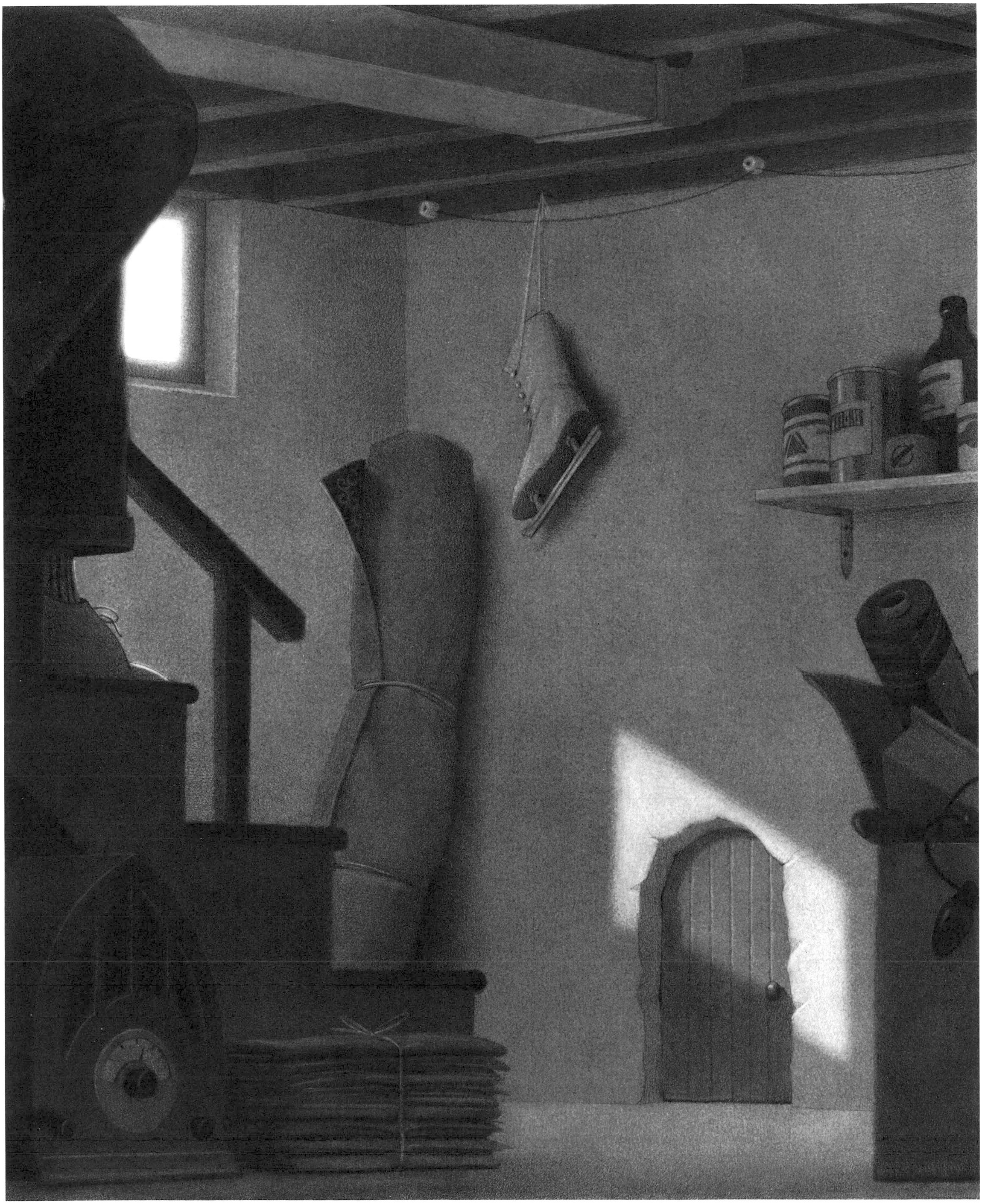

THE HARP

So it's true he thought, it's really true.

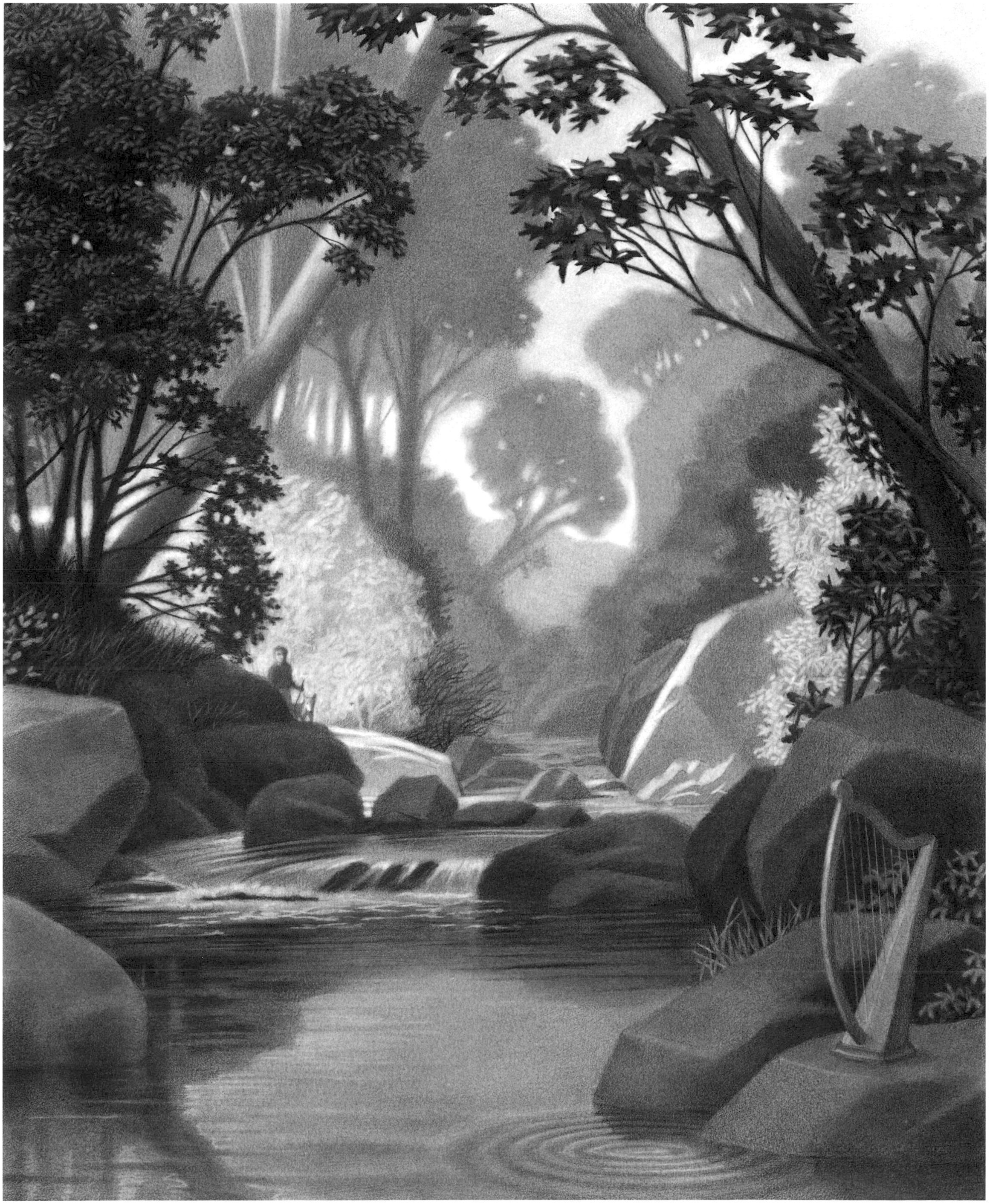

MR. LINDEN'S LIBRARY

He had warned her about the book.
Now it was too late.

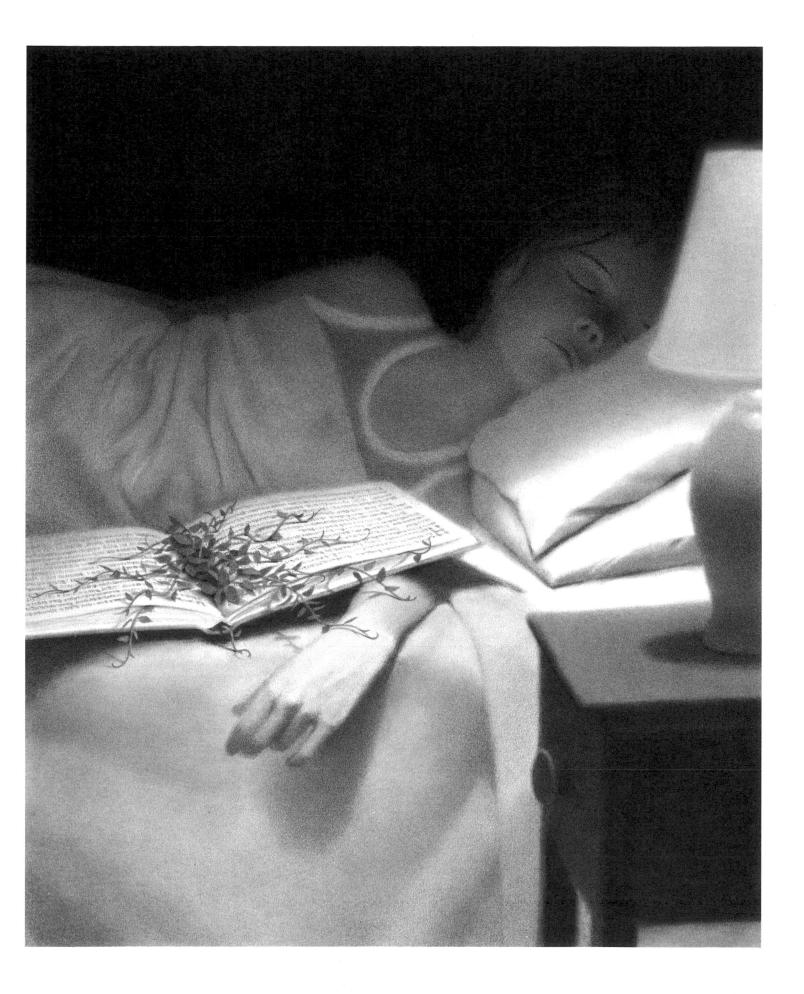

THE SEVEN CHAIRS

The fifth one ended up in France.

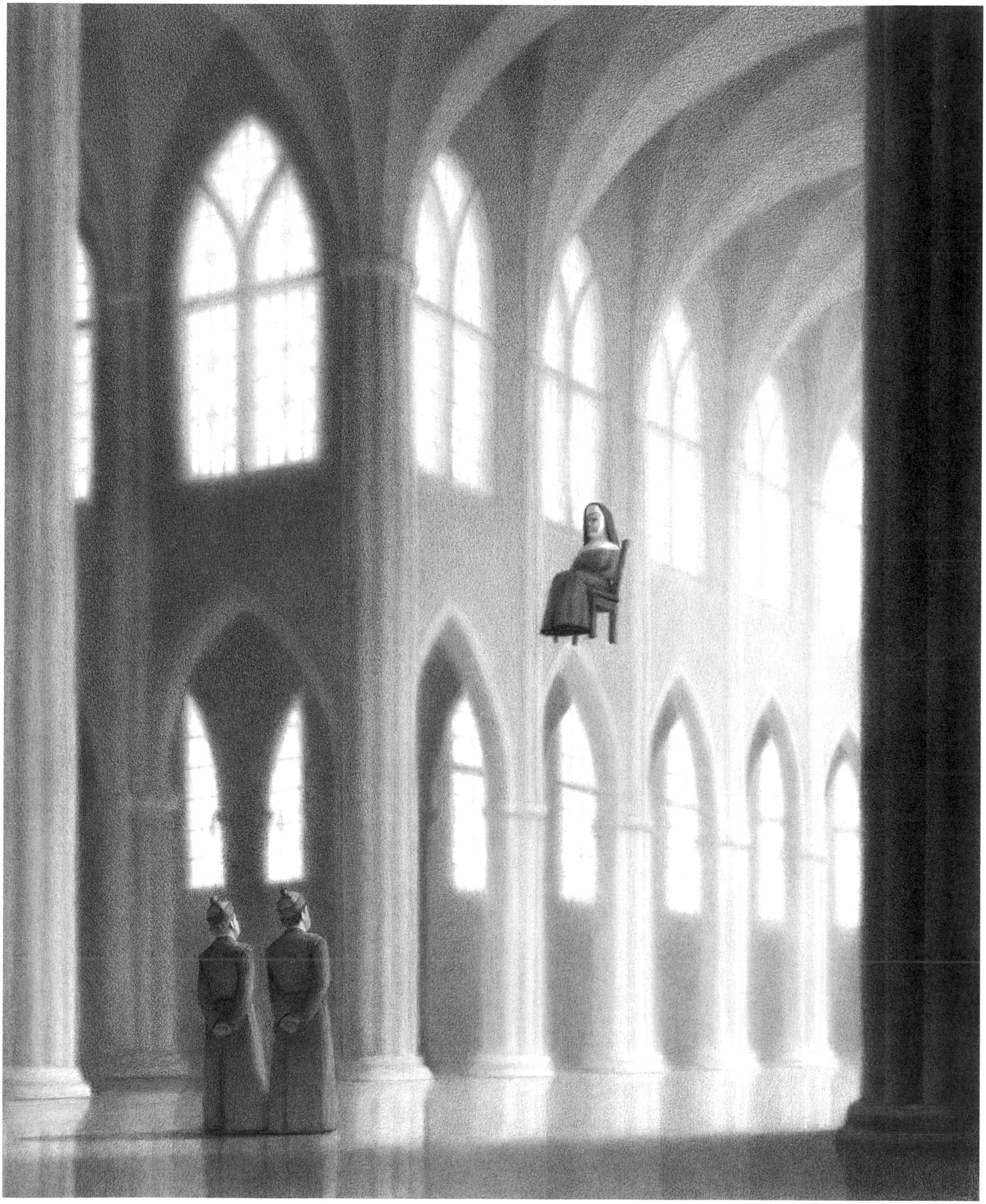

THE THIRD-FLOOR BEDROOM

*It all began when someone left
the window open.*

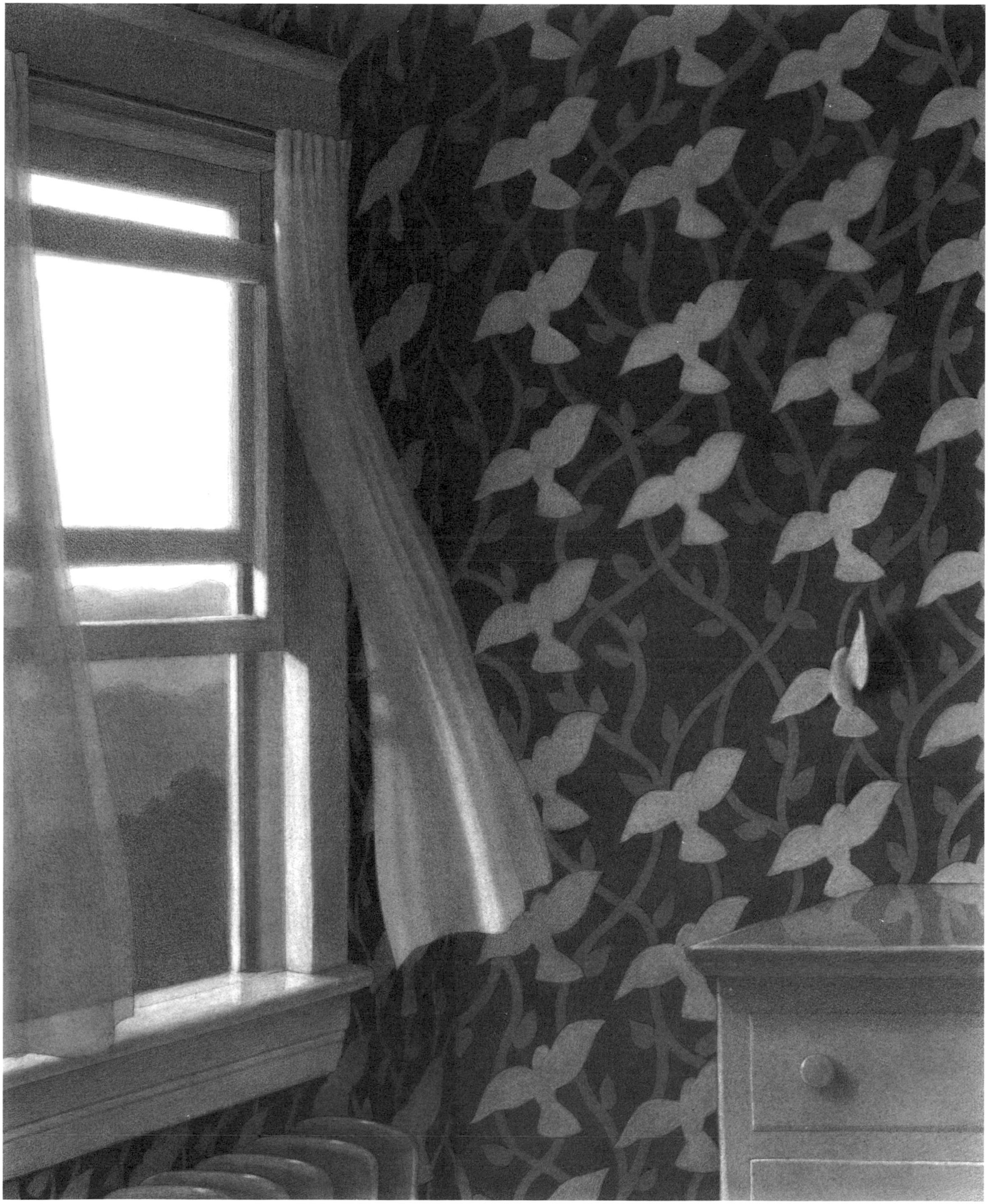

JUST DESERT

She lowered the knife and
it grew even brighter.

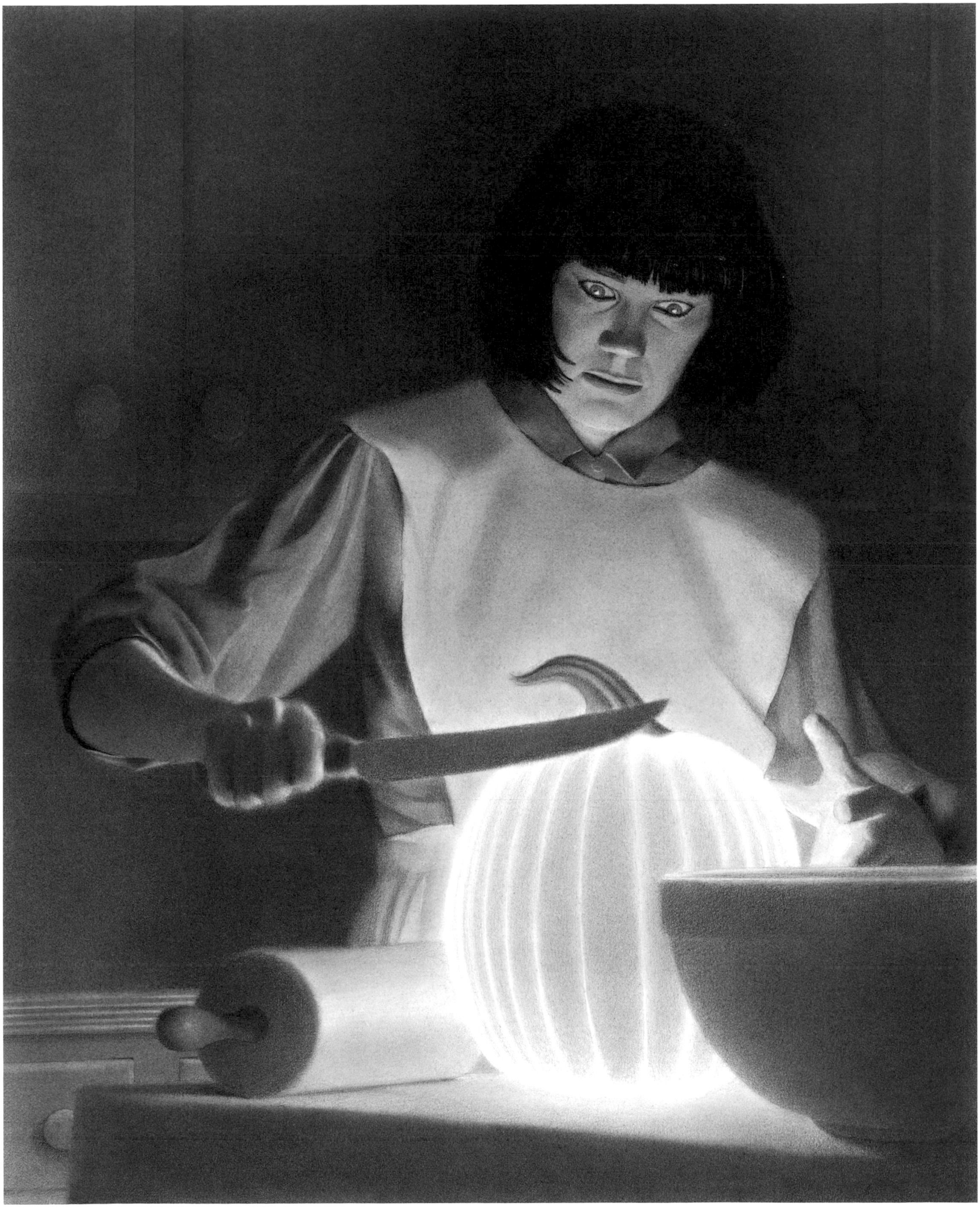

CAPTAIN TORY

He swung his lantern
three times and slowly the schooner appeared.

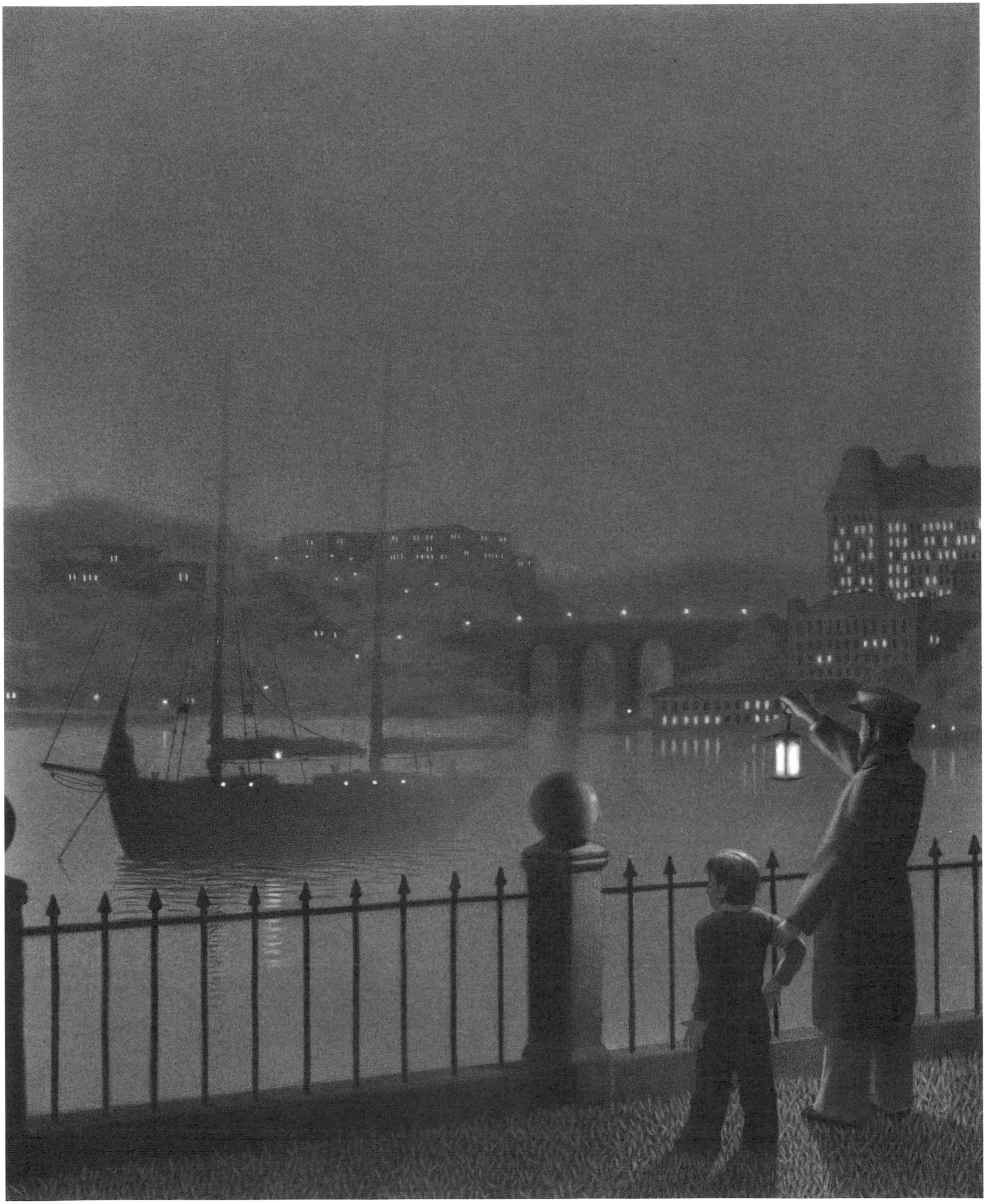

OSCAR AND ALPHONSE

She knew it was time to send them back.
The caterpillars softly wiggled in her hand,
spelling out "goodbye."

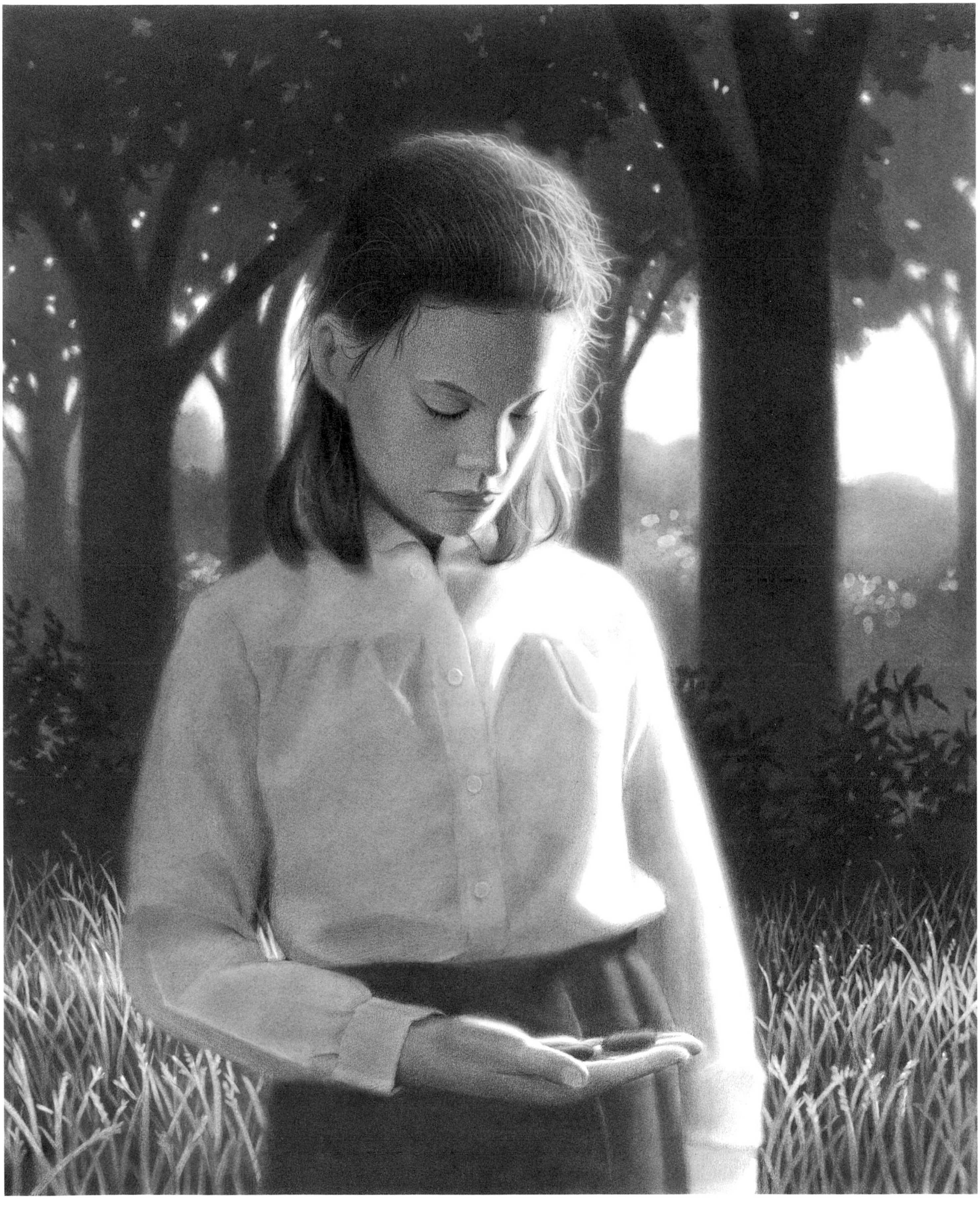

THE HOUSE ON MAPLE STREET

It was a perfect lift-off.

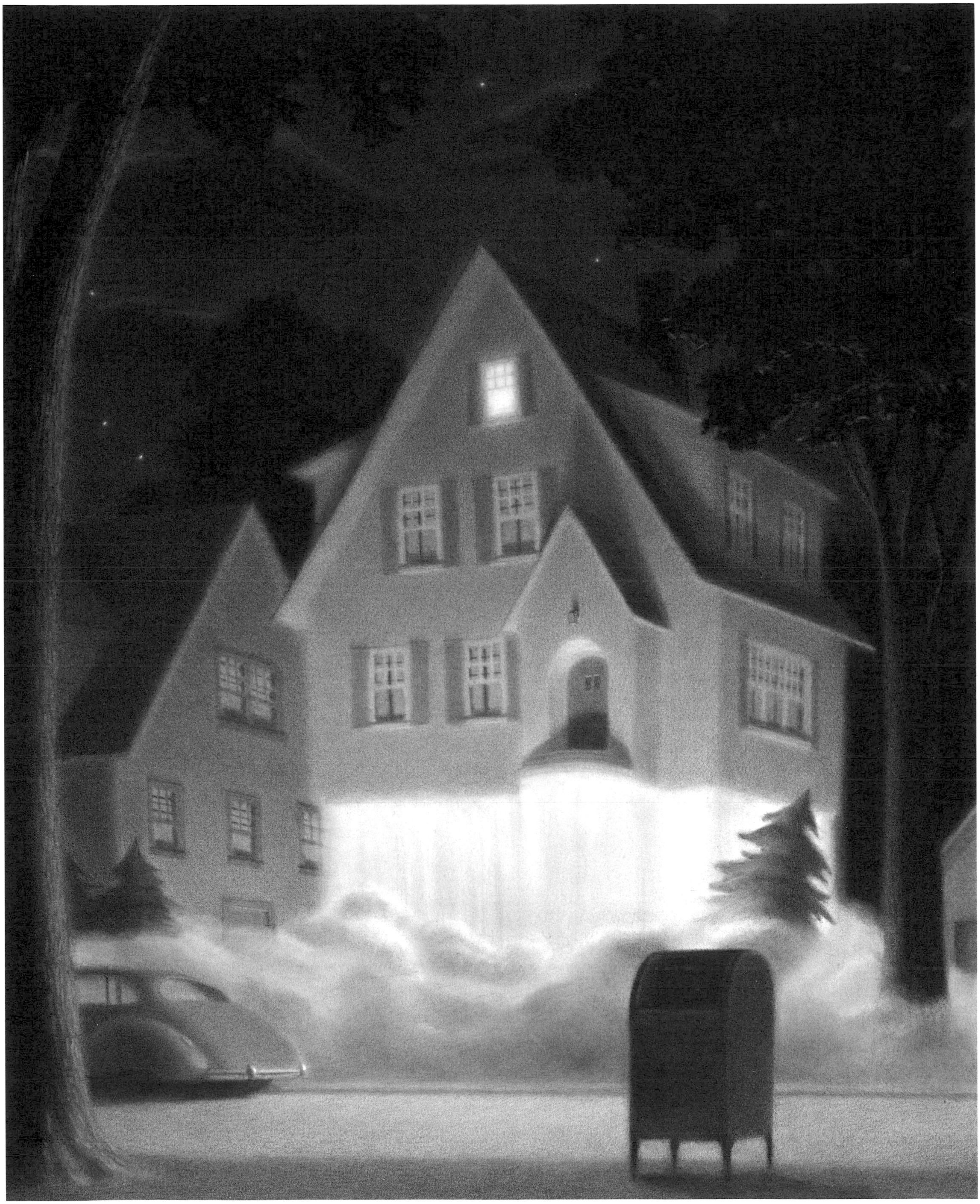